Snow

CYNTHIA RYLANT

Snow

ILLUSTRATED BY
LAUREN STRINGER

Houghton Mifflin Harcourt
Boston   New York

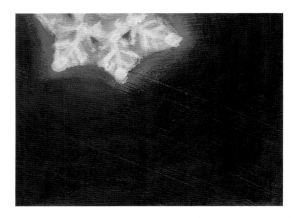

The illustrations in this book were done in acrylic paints on Arches 140 lb. watercolor paper.
The display lettering was created by Monica Dengo.
The text type was set in Perpetua.

The Library of Congress has cataloged the hardcover edition as follows:
Rylant, Cynthia.
Snow / [text by] Cynthia Rylant; [illustrated by] Lauren Stringer.
p. cm.
Summary: Celebrates the beauty of a snowfall and its happy effects on children.
[1. Snow—Fiction.] I. Stringer, Lauren, ill. II. Title.
PZ7.R982Sn   2008
[E]—dc22 2006006171

ISBN: 978-0-15-205303-1 hardcover
ISBN: 978-1-328-74055-7 paperback

Manufactured in China
SCP 10 9 8 7 6 5 4
4500741674

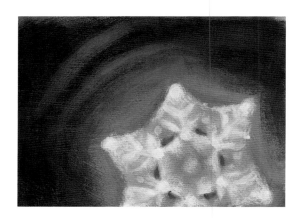

For my sister, Merrill, and my brother, Dave,
and all that we remember

—L.S.

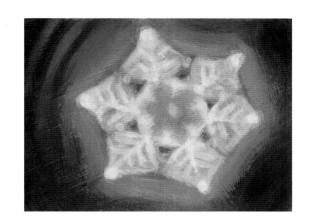

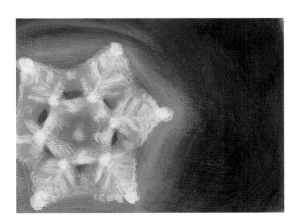

The best snow
is the snow that
comes softly in the night,
like a shy friend
afraid to knock,
so she thinks she'll
just wait in the yard
until you see her.
This is the snow
that brings you peace.

And then there is the snow
that begins to fall
in fat, cheerful flakes
while you are somewhere
you'd rather not be.
Maybe school.
Maybe work.

And this snow
tells you, as it falls, that
it will send you home early,
don't worry.
Home is where you
need to be,
and this snow
will take you there.

It will send you back,
over slippery white roads,
to the rooms you love so well.
And it will say
that it is all right
to be happy.

Some snows fall only lightly,
just enough
to make you notice
the delicate limbs of trees,
the light falling
from the lamppost,
a sparrow's small feet.

And some snows fall so heavy
they bury
cars up to their noses,
and make evergreens bow,
and keep your kitties
curled up awhile.

Children love snow
better than anyone does,
and they never complain
as they pull on their
red boots and mittens
and make plans
to catch
wet flakes on their tongues

and roll their small bodies
to the bottom of a hill.

The snow loves them back.
It gives them angels

and new friends.

And the snow,
while it is here,
reminds us of this:
that nothing lasts forever
except memories.

And while the snow
is here
this brief moment,
let us take a walk
and see how beautiful
the world is

and then come back
to our white, quiet homes
and make something
warm to drink
and maybe read
or play a game
or tell each other
all that
we've been thinking.

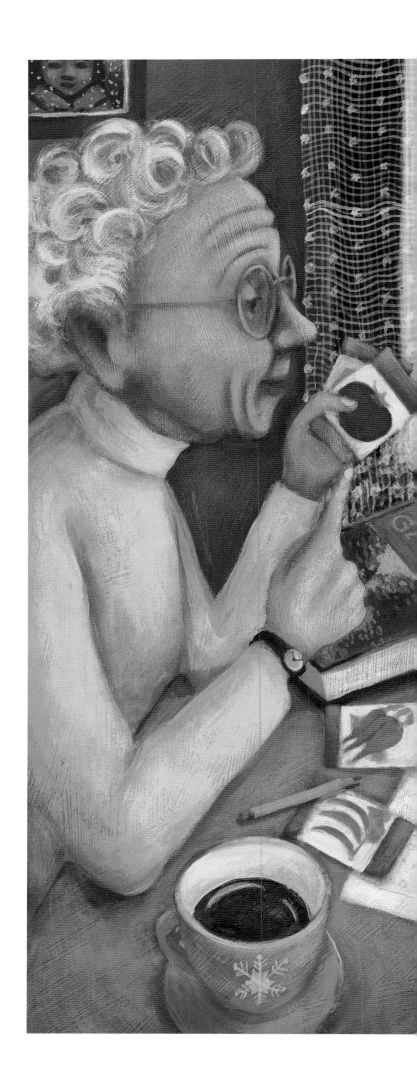

The snow is falling
while the flowers sleep
and the sun sleeps
and the soft green gardens
are waiting.

It is the snow's turn now.

We'll watch it fall.

CYNTHIA RYLANT fell in love with the snow when she was a child in rural Appalachia. She is the author of more than a hundred books for young people, including the Mr. Putter & Tabby beginning reader series and the novel *Missing May,* which received the Newbery Medal. She lives in Lake Oswego, Oregon.

LAUREN STRINGER's paintings for *Snow* were inspired by the memories of three generations of her family growing up in snowy Minnesota. She has illustrated many acclaimed picture books, including *Scarecrow* by Cynthia Rylant, *Mud* by Mary Lyn Ray, and her own *Winter Is the Warmest Season.* She lives in Minneapolis. Visit her website at www.laurenstringer.com.